Deric the Child Spitter

by Dr. Mills

Illustrated By Nicolas Lonprez

In a white house on a big hill
With a big dog named Bach
Lived a little girl named Gracie
Who was curiously smart
Gracie was a good girl
But on occasion she slipped
When adventure came calling
She just could not resist

After many years exploring
The yard of the back
It was time to expand
To a front yard attack

Then one day at the front gate
She pushed and fell through
The front yard was calling
So what could she do?

She climbed into mommies car
And let the park brake go free
Then steered that big car
Down the big hill into a tree

When Daddy got home
He was very glad she wasn't hurt
But he sure did look angry
When he surveyed Gracie's work

The front gate, now locked up
The front yard out of bounds
Gracie got curious
About the subterranean grounds

Daddy worked downstairs
In his dark basement lair
Gracie would visit
To investigate down there

On her latest investigation
A secret door Gracie spied
She pushed and it opened
Slowly peering inside

Temptation extreme
And although she was wary
Gracie crept in
To the damp, dark and scary

Up the dirt steps
One step at a time
Shakily Gracie
Heard a noise from behind

It happened so fast
It frightened her so
It had her by the ankle
And it wouldn't let go

It dragged her back out
Voice growlie and low
"Why are you in here?
It's dangerous you know"

Suddenly Gracie
Was frozen in fright
The thing that had grabbed her
Was fierce alright
Timidly she turned
To view the creature attacking
And above her stood Daddy
Arms folded, foot tapping

"Under the house
Is a place not to go
There are very frightening things
In the darkness you know"

"What things are in there?"
Gracie asked, face still white
"Things that can harm you
Things that creep in the night"
"Well I want to see one
These things sound OK
How bad could they be?
Are they there in the day?"

"Well there's one thing for sure
That you don't want to meet
He has evil red eyes
And tentically feet
He makes disgusting mouth noises
And spits green slimey slime
He eats naughty children
In the dark all the time"

"And when he eats children
He cooks them with butter"
"Wh wh what is his name?"
Gracie asked with a stutter
"It starts with a D
And is followed by Eric
The D stands for DARK
But just call him Deric"

"Dark Eric The Child Spitter
Is the name he was born with
He has teeth like swords
Which children can be torn with "

So Gracie never ever
Went back through that door
She'd dream about Deric
Living under her floor

Gracie's grown up now
And has kids of her own
But Deric still visits
When she's
IN THE DARK...
Alone

ABOUT THE AUTHOR

Dr. Simon E. Mills is an Australian born, internationally published author, musician, song writer, business man and entrepreneur.
Dr. Mills now lives in New York City with his wife and three children who are often the inspiration behind his stories.

www.SimonMills.com

OTHER TITLES BY THE AUTHOR

www.SimonMills.com/books